THERE'S A FLY GUY IN MY SOUP

Tedd Arnold

Cartwheel Books • New York

An Imprint of Scholastic Inc.

Specially for the Beecher Doll Club
and everyone at the Arnot Art Museum

Library of Congress Cataloging-in-Publication Data

Arnold, Tedd.
There's a Fly Guy in my soup / Tedd Arnold.
p. cm. -- (Fly Guy ; 12)
Summary: When Fly Guy is not allowed in the restaurant with Buzz's
family he follows his nose and ends up in the soup.
ISBN 978-0-545-31284-4
1. Restaurants--Juvenile fiction. 2. Flies--Juvenile fiction. [1.
Restaurants--Fiction. 2. Flies--Fiction.] I. Title. II. Title: There is
a Fly Guy in my soup. III. Series: Arnold, Tedd. Fly Guy ; #12.

PZ7.A7379Thm 2012
[E]--dc23

2012000801

ISBN 978-0-545-31284-4

10 9 8 7 6 5 4 3 2 1   12 13 14 15 16 17

Printed in China 38

First edition, September 2012

A boy had a pet fly.
He named him Fly Guy.
And Fly Guy could
say the boy's name—

BUZZ!

Chapter 1

One day, Fly Guy went with Buzz, Mom, and Dad on a long trip.

They drove until dinnertime.
They stopped at a hotel.
"Yay!" said Buzz. "I love hotels!"

"Cool room," said Buzz.
"Time for dinner," said Dad.
"There is a nice restaurant
downstairs," said Mom,
"but Fly Guy can't go there."

"Fly Guy can eat outside," said Buzz. "Right, Fly Guy?"

Fly Guy flew outside.

He found a
trash can.

He found
a puddle.

He found a sticky spot.

He found the biggest, slimiest
garbage can ever.

But he didn't find anything that he wanted to eat.

Chapter 2

Then Fly Guy smelled
something wonderful.

Fly Guy followed the smell.

At last, he found where he
wanted to eat!

Fly Guy needed to wash
before dinner.

He spied a small round
bathtub with warm
brown water. Perfect!

Fly Guy jumped in.

He washed his face and hands.

He washed his armpits.

He washed between his toes.

Chapter 3

Fly Guy's bathtub was picked up and carried to another room.

It was set down on a table
in front of a lady.

The lady screamed, "Waiter! There's a fly in my soup!"

The lady jumped up. Her soup and Fly Guy went flying...

...into another lady's soup.

That lady jumped up. Her soup
and the first lady's soup
and Fly Guy went flying...

...onto a gentleman's head.

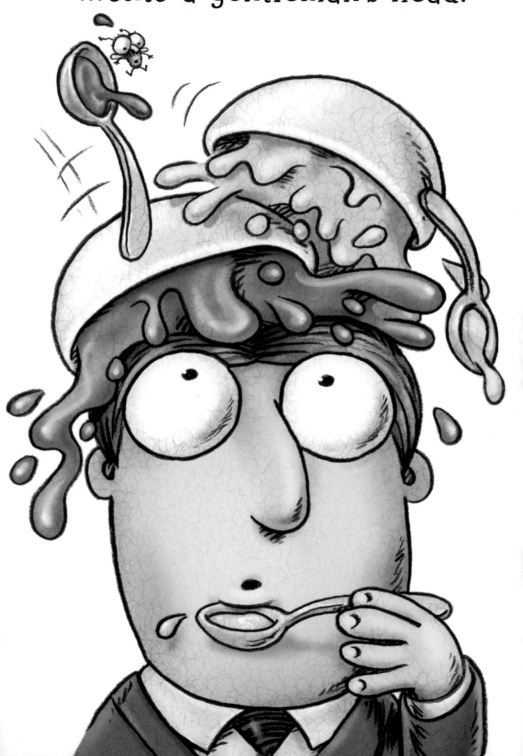

The gentleman jumped up.
The soup and Fly Guy
and the gentleman's hair
went flying....

Everyone jumped up. Everyone's soup and Fly Guy and the gentleman's hair went flying.

Fly Guy still needed a bath.
Buzz, Mom, and Dad
needed a bath.

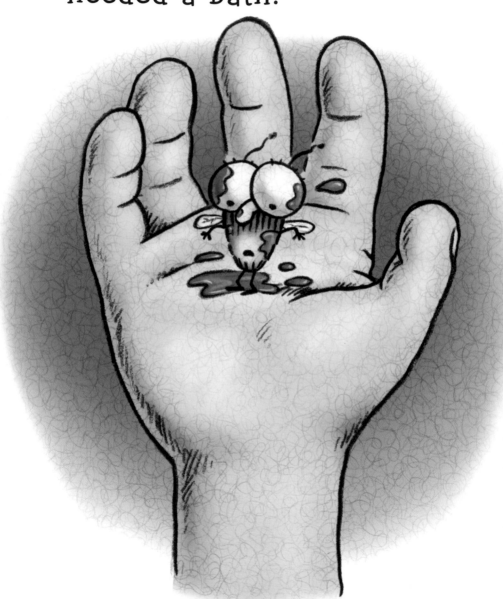

Everyone needed a bath.
"Last one in the pool is a
rotten egg!" yelled Buzz.